DREAM LIFE
AND REAL LIFE

A LITTLE AFRICAN STORY

By

OLIVE SCHREINER

First published in 1893

Read & Co.

Dedication to

My Brother Fred,

For Whose Little School Magazine the First of
These Tiny Stories—One of the First I Ever Made—
was Written out Many Long Years Ago

O. S.
New College, Eastbourne,
Sept. 29, 1893

CONTENTS

Olive Schreiner

Olive Schreiner was born on Wittebergen Reserve, Cape Colony (present-day Lesotho) in 1855. After finishing school, she found work as a governess and a schoolteacher, and during her free time began to work on a novel about her experiences in South Africa.

When Schreiner had saved enough money, she travelled to Britain, hoping to become a doctor. She lived in London where she began attending lectures at the Medical School, as well as attending socialist meetings. Schreiner met the publisher George Meredith, who in 1883 published her best-known novel, *Story of an African Farm*. A commercial and critical success, it is now seen as a defining work of early feminism – as is her later work, *Women and Labour* (1911).

Over the rest of her life, Schreiner made the acquaintance of a number of figures in London society, including future Prime Minister William Gladstone. In 1889, she returned to South Africa to be with her family. Her brother, William Schreiner, later became prime minister of Cape Colony. Over the next few years she published two collections of short stories, *Dreams* (1891) and *Dream Life and Real Life* (1893). She also became heavily involved in politics, and was a fierce opponent of racism and imperialism. Her 1897 work *Trooper Peter Halkett of Mashonaland* (1897) was a strong attack on British rule in South Africa.

At the outbreak of the First World War, Schreiner moved back to Britain. Over the next four years she was active in the peace movement and worked closely with organizations such as the Union of Democratic Control and the Non-Conscription Fellowship. She returned to South Africa in of August 1920, and dying following a heart attack later that year.

KOPJES—In the karoo, are hillocks of stones, that rise up singly or in clusters, here and there; presenting sometimes the fantastic appearance of old ruined castles or giant graves, the work of human hands.

KRAAL—A sheepfold.

KRANTZ—A precipice.

SLUIT—A deep fissure, generally dry, in which the superfluous torrents of water are carried from the karoo plains after thunderstorms.

STOEP—A porch.

I

DREAM LIFE AND REAL LIFE; A LITTLE AFRICAN STORY

Little Jannita sat alone beside a milk-bush. Before her and behind her stretched the plain, covered with red sand and thorny karoo bushes; and here and there a milk-bush, looking like a bundle of pale green rods tied together. Not a tree was to be seen anywhere, except on the banks of the river, and that was far away, and the sun beat on her head. Round her fed the Angora goats she was herding; pretty things, especially the little ones, with white silky curls that touched the ground. But Jannita sat crying. If an angel should gather up in his cup all the tears that have been shed, I think the bitterest would be those of children.

By and by she was so tired, and the sun was so hot, she laid her head against the milk-bush, and dropped asleep.

She dreamed a beautiful dream. She thought that when she went back to the farmhouse in the evening, the walls were covered with vines and roses, and the kraals were not made of red stone, but of lilac trees full of blossom. And the fat old Boer smiled at her; and the stick he held across the door, for the goats to jump over, was a lily rod with seven blossoms at the end. When she went to the house her mistress gave her a whole roaster-cake for her supper, and the mistress's daughter had stuck a rose in the cake; and her mistress's son-in-law said, "Thank you!" when she pulled off his boots, and did not kick her.

It was a beautiful dream.

While she lay thus dreaming, one of the little kids came and licked her on her cheek, because of the salt from her dried-up tears. And in her dream she was not a poor indentured child any more, living with Boers. It was her father who kissed her. He said he had only been asleep—that day when he lay down under the thorn-bush; he had not really died. He felt her hair, and said it was grown long and silky, and he said they would go back to Denmark now. He asked her why her feet were bare, and what the marks on her back were. Then he put her head on his shoulder, and picked her up, and carried her away, away! She laughed—she could feel her face against his brown beard. His arms were so strong.

As she lay there dreaming, with the ants running over her naked feet, and with her brown curls lying in the sand, a Hottentot came up to her. He was dressed in ragged yellow trousers, and a dirty shirt, and torn jacket. He had a red handkerchief round his head, and a felt hat above that. His nose was flat, his eyes like slits, and the wool on his head was gathered into little round balls. He came to the milk-bush, and looked at the little girl lying in the hot sun. Then he walked off, and caught one of the fattest little Angora goats, and held its mouth fast, as he stuck it under his arm. He looked back to see that she was still sleeping, and jumped down into one of the sluits. He walked down the bed of the sluit a little way and came to an overhanging bank, under which, sitting on the red sand, were two men. One was a tiny, ragged, old bushman, four feet high; the other was an English navvy, in a dark blue blouse. They cut the kid's throat with the navvy's long knife, and covered up the blood with sand, and buried the entrails and skin. Then they talked, and quarrelled a little; and then they talked quietly again.

The Hottentot man put a leg of the kid under his coat and left the rest of the meat for the two in the sluit, and walked away.

When little Jannita awoke it was almost sunset. She sat up very frightened, but her goats were all about her. She began to drive them home. "I do not think there are any lost," she said.

Dirk, the Hottentot, had brought his flock home already, and stood at the kraal door with his ragged yellow trousers. The fat old Boer put his stick across the door, and let Jannita's goats jump over, one by one. He counted them. When the last jumped over: "Have you been to sleep today?" he said; "there is one missing."

Then little Jannita knew what was coming, and she said, in a low voice, "No." And then she felt in her heart that deadly sickness that you feel when you tell a lie; and again she said, "Yes."

"Do you think you will have any supper this evening?" said the Boer.

"No," said Jannita.

"What do you think you will have?"

"I don't know," said Jannita.

"Give me your whip," said the Boer to Dirk, the Hottentot.

* * * * *

The moon was all but full that night. Oh, but its light was beautiful!

The little girl crept to the door of the outhouse where she slept, and looked at it. When you are hungry, and very, very sore, you do not cry. She leaned her chin on one hand, and looked, with her great dove's eyes—the other hand was cut open, so she wrapped it in her pinafore. She looked across the plain at the sand and the low karoo-bushes, with the moonlight on them.

Presently, there came slowly, from far away, a wild springbuck. It came close to the house, and stood looking at it in wonder, while the moonlight glinted on its horns, and in its great eyes. It stood wondering at the red brick walls, and the girl watched it. Then, suddenly, as if it scorned it all, it curved its beautiful back and turned; and away it fled over the bushes and sand, like a sheeny streak of white lightning. She stood up to watch it. So free, so free! Away, away! She watched, till she could see it no more on the wide plain.

Her heart swelled, larger, larger, larger: she uttered a low cry; and without waiting, pausing, thinking, she followed on its track. Away, away, away! "I—I also!" she said, "I—I also!"

When at last her legs began to tremble under her, and she stopped to breathe, the house was a speck behind her. She dropped on the earth, and held her panting sides.

She began to think now.

If she stayed on the plain they would trace her footsteps in the morning and catch her; but if she waded in the water in the bed of the river they would not be able to find her footmarks; and she would hide, there where the rocks and the kopjes were.

So she stood up and walked towards the river. The water in the river was low; just a line of silver in the broad bed of sand, here and there broadening into a pool. She stepped into it, and bathed her feet in the delicious cold water. Up and up the stream she walked, where it rattled over the pebbles, and past where the farmhouse lay; and where the rocks were large she leaped from one to the other. The night wind in her face made her strong—she laughed. She had never felt such night wind before. So the night smells to the wild bucks, because they are free! A free thing feels as a chained thing never can.

At last she came to a place where the willows grew on each side of the river, and trailed their long branches on the sandy bed. She could not tell why, she could not tell the reason, but a feeling of fear came over her.

On the left bank rose a chain of kopjes and a precipice of rocks. Between the precipice and the river bank there was a narrow path covered by the fragments of fallen rock. And upon the summit of the precipice a kippersol tree grew, whose palm-like leaves were clearly cut out against the night sky. The rocks cast a deep shadow, and the willow trees, on either side of the river. She paused, looked up and about her, and then ran on, fearful.

"What was I afraid of? How foolish I have been!" she said, when she came to a place where the trees were not so close together. And she stood still and looked back and shivered.

At last her steps grew wearier and wearier. She was very sleepy now, she could scarcely lift her feet. She stepped out of the river-bed. She only saw that the rocks about her were wild, as though many little kopjes had been broken up and strewn upon the ground, lay down at the foot of an aloe, and fell asleep.

* * * * *

But, in the morning, she saw what a glorious place it was. The rocks were piled on one another, and tossed this way and that. Prickly pears grew among them, and there were no less than six kippersol trees scattered here and there among the broken kopjes. In the rocks there were hundreds of homes for the conies, and from the crevices wild asparagus hung down. She ran to the river, bathed in the clear cold water, and tossed it over her head. She sang aloud. All the songs she knew were sad, so she could not sing them now, she was glad, she was so free; but she sang the notes without the words, as the cock-o-veets do. Singing and jumping all the way, she went back, and took a sharp stone, and cut at the root of a kippersol, and got out a large piece, as long as her arm, and sat to chew it. Two conies came out on the rock above her head and peeped at her. She held them out a piece, but they did not want it, and ran away.

It was very delicious to her. Kippersol is like raw quince, when it is very green; but she liked it. When good food is thrown at you by other people, strange to say, it is very bitter; but whatever you find yourself is sweet!

When she had finished she dug out another piece, and went to look for a pantry to put it in. At the top of a heap of rocks up which she clambered she found that some large stones stood apart but met at the top, making a room.

"Oh, this is my little home!" she said.

At the top and all round it was closed, only in the front it was open. There was a beautiful shelf in the wall for the kippersol, and she scrambled down again. She brought a great bunch of prickly pear, and stuck it in a crevice before the door, and hung wild asparagus over it, till it looked as though it grew there. No one could see that there was a room there, for she left only a tiny opening, and hung a branch of feathery asparagus over it. Then she crept in to see how it looked. There was a glorious soft green light. Then she went out and picked some of those purple little ground flowers—you know them—those that keep their faces close to the ground, but when you turn them up and look at them they are deep blue eyes looking into yours! She took them with a little earth, and put them in the crevices between the rocks; and so the room was quite furnished. Afterwards she went down to the river and brought her arms full of willow, and made a lovely bed; and, because the weather was very hot, she lay down to rest upon it.

She went to sleep soon, and slept long, for she was very weak. Late in the afternoon she was awakened by a few cold drops falling on her face. She sat up. A great and fierce thunderstorm had been raging, and a few of the cool drops had fallen through the crevice in the rocks. She pushed the asparagus branch aside, and looked out, with her little hands folded about her knees. She heard the thunder rolling, and saw the red torrents rush among the stones on their way to the river. She heard the roar of the river as it now rolled, angry and red, bearing away stumps and trees on its muddy water. She listened and smiled, and pressed closer to the rock that took care of her. She pressed the palm of her hand against it. When you have no one to love you, you love the dumb things very much. When the sun set, it cleared up. Then the little girl ate some kippersol, and lay down again to sleep. She thought there was nothing so nice as to sleep. When one has had no food but kippersol juice for two days, one doesn't feel strong.

"It is so nice here," she thought as she went to sleep, "I will stay here always."

Afterwards the moon rose. The sky was very clear now, there was not a cloud anywhere; and the moon shone in through the bushes in the door, and made a lattice-work of light on her face. She was dreaming a beautiful dream. The loveliest dreams of all are dreamed when you are hungry. She thought she was walking in a beautiful place, holding her father's hand, and they both had crowns on their heads, crowns of wild asparagus. The people whom they passed smiled and kissed her; some gave her flowers, and some gave her food, and the sunlight was everywhere. She dreamed the same dream over and over, and it grew more and more beautiful; till, suddenly, it seemed as though she were standing quite alone. She looked up: on one side of her was the high precipice, on the other was the river, with the willow trees, drooping their branches into the water; and the moonlight was over all. Up, against the night sky the pointed leaves of the kippersol trees were clearly marked, and the rocks and the willow trees cast dark shadows.

In her sleep she shivered, and half awoke.

"Ah, I am not there, I am here," she said; and she crept closer to the rock, and kissed it, and went to sleep again.

It must have been about three o'clock, for the moon had begun to sink towards the western sky, when she woke, with a violent start. She sat up, and pressed her hand against her heart.

"What can it be? A cony must surely have run across my feet and frightened me!" she said, and she turned to lie down again; but soon she sat up. Outside, there was the distinct sound of thorns crackling in a fire.

She crept to the door and made an opening in the branches with her fingers.

A large fire was blazing in the shadow, at the foot of the rocks. A little Bushman sat over some burning coals that had been raked from it, cooking meat. Stretched on the ground was an Englishman, dressed in a blouse, and with a heavy, sullen face. On the stone beside him was Dirk, the Hottentot, sharpening a bowie knife.

She held her breath. Not a cony in all the rocks was so still.

"They can never find me here," she said; and she knelt, and listened to every word they said. She could hear it all.

"You may have all the money," said the Bushman; "but I want the cask of brandy. I will set the roof alight in six places, for a Dutchman burnt my mother once alive in a hut, with three children."

"You are sure there is no one else on the farm?" said the navvy.

"No, I have told you till I am tired," said Dirk; "The two Kaffirs have gone with the son to town; and the maids have gone to a dance; there is only the old man and the two women left."

"But suppose," said the navvy, "he should have the gun at his bedside, and loaded!"

"He never has," said Dirk; "it hangs in the passage, and the cartridges too. He never thought when he bought it what work it was for! I only wish the little white girl was there still," said Dirk; "but she is drowned. We traced her footmarks to the great pool that has no bottom."

She listened to every word, and they talked on.

Afterwards, the little Bushman, who crouched over the fire, sat up suddenly, listening.

"Ha! what is that?" he said.

A Bushman is like a dog: his ear is so fine he knows a jackal's tread from a wild dog's.

"I heard nothing," said the navvy.

"I heard," said the Hottentot; "but it was only a cony on the rocks."

"No cony, no cony," said the Bushman; "see, what is that there moving in the shade round the point?"

"Nothing, you idiot!" said the navvy. "Finish your meat; we must start now."

There were two roads to the homestead. One went along the open plain, and was by far the shortest; but you might be seen half a mile off. The other ran along the river bank, where there were rocks, and holes, and willow trees to hide among. And all down the river bank ran a little figure.

The river was swollen by the storm full to its banks, and the willow trees dipped their half-drowned branches into its water. Wherever there was a gap between them, you could see it flow, red and muddy, with the stumps upon it. But the little figure ran on and on; never looking, never thinking; panting, panting! There, where the rocks were the thickest; there, where on the open space the moonlight shone; there, where the prickly pears were tangled, and the rocks cast shadows, on it ran; the little hands clinched, the little heart beating, the eyes fixed always ahead.

It was not far to run now. Only the narrow path between the high rocks and the river.

At last she came to the end of it, and stood for an instant. Before her lay the plain, and the red farmhouse, so near, that if persons had been walking there you might have seen them in the moonlight. She clasped her hands. "Yes, I will tell them, I will tell them!" she said; "I am almost there!" She ran forward again, then hesitated. She shaded her eyes from the moonlight, and looked. Between her and the farmhouse there were three figures moving over the low bushes.

In the sheeny moonlight you could see how they moved on, slowly and furtively; the short one, and the one in light clothes, and the one in dark.

"I cannot help them now!" she cried, and sank down on the ground, with her little hands clasped before her.

* * * * *

"Awake, awake!" said the farmer's wife; "I hear a strange noise; something calling, calling, calling!"

The man rose, and went to the window.

"I hear it also," he said; "surely some jackal's at the sheep. I will load my gun and go and see."

"It sounds to me like the cry of no jackal," said the woman; and when he was gone she woke her daughter.

"Come, let us go and make a fire, I can sleep no more," she said; "I have heard a strange thing tonight. Your father said it was a jackal's cry, but no jackal cries so. It was a child's voice, and it cried, 'Master, master, wake!'"

The women looked at each other; then they went to the kitchen, and made a great fire; and they sang psalms all the while.

At last the man came back; and they asked him, "What have you seen?" "Nothing," he said, "but the sheep asleep in their kraals, and the moonlight on the walls. And yet, it did seem to me," he added, "that far away near the krantz by the river, I saw three figures moving. And afterwards—it might have been fancy—I thought I heard the cry again; but since that, all has been still there."

* * * * *

Next day a navvy had returned to the railway works.

"Where have you been so long?" his comrades asked.

"He keeps looking over his shoulder," said one, "as though he thought he should see something there."

"When he drank his grog today," said another, "he let it fall, and looked round."

Next day, a small old Bushman, and a Hottentot, in ragged yellow trousers, were at a wayside canteen. When the Bushman had had brandy, he began to tell how something (he did not say whether it was man, woman, or child) had lifted up its hands and cried for mercy; had kissed a white man's hands, and cried to him to help it. Then the Hottentot took the Bushman by the throat, and dragged him out.

Next night, the moon rose up, and mounted the quiet sky. She was full now, and looked in at the little home; at the purple flowers stuck about the room, and the kippersol on the shelf.

Her light fell on the willow trees, and on the high rocks, and on a little new-made heap of earth and round stones. Three men knew what was under it; and no one else ever will.

Lily Kloof, South Africa.

II

THE WOMAN'S ROSE

I have an old, brown carved box; the lid is broken and tied with a string. In it I keep little squares of paper, with hair inside, and a little picture which hung over my brother's bed when we were children, and other things as small. I have in it a rose. Other women also have such boxes where they keep such trifles, but no one has my rose.

When my eye is dim, and my heart grows faint, and my faith in woman flickers, and her present is an agony to me, and her future a despair, the scent of that dead rose, withered for twelve years, comes back to me. I know there will be spring; as surely as the birds know it when they see above the snow two tiny, quivering green leaves. Spring cannot fail us.

There were other flowers in the box once; a bunch of white acacia flowers, gathered by the strong hand of a man, as we passed down a village street on a sultry afternoon, when it had rained, and the drops fell on us from the leaves of the acacia trees. The flowers were damp; they made mildew marks on the paper I folded them in. After many years I threw them away. There is nothing of them left in the box now, but a faint, strong smell of dried acacia, that recalls that sultry summer afternoon; but the rose is in the box still.

It is many years ago now; I was a girl of fifteen, and I went to visit in a small up-country town. It was young in those days, and two days' journey from the nearest village; the population consisted mainly of men. A few were married, and had their wives and children, but most were single. There was only one young girl there when I came. She was about seventeen, fair, and rather fully-fleshed; she had large dreamy blue eyes, and wavy light hair; full, rather heavy lips, until she smiled; then her face broke into dimples, and all her white teeth shone. The hotel-keeper may have had a daughter, and the farmer in the outskirts had two, but we never saw them. She reigned alone. All the men worshipped her. She was the only woman they had to think of. They talked of her on the stoep, at the market, at the hotel; they watched for her at street corners; they hated the man she bowed to or walked with down the street. They brought flowers to the front door; they offered her their horses; they begged her to marry them when they dared. Partly, there was something noble and heroic in this devotion of men to the best woman they knew; partly there was something natural in it, that these men, shut off from the world, should pour at the feet of one woman the worship that otherwise would have been given to twenty; and partly there was something mean in their envy of one another. If she had raised her little finger, I suppose, she might have married any one out of twenty of them.

Then I came. I do not think I was prettier; I do not think I was so pretty as she was. I was certainly not as handsome. But I was vital, and I was new, and she was old—they all forsook her and followed me. They worshipped me. It was to my door that the flowers came; it was I had twenty horses offered me when I could only ride one; it was for me they waited at street corners; it was what I said and did that they talked of. Partly I liked it. I had lived alone all my life; no one ever had told me I was beautiful and a woman. I believed them. I did not know it was simply a fashion, which one man had set and the rest followed unreasoningly. I liked them to ask me to marry them, and to say, No. I despised them. The mother heart had not swelled in me yet; I did not know all men were my children, as the large woman knows when her heart is grown. I was too small to be tender. I liked my power. I was like a child with a new whip, which it goes about cracking everywhere, not caring against what. I could not wind it up and put it away. Men were curious creatures, who liked me, I could never tell why. Only one thing took from my pleasure; I could not bear that they had deserted her for me. I liked her great dreamy blue eyes, I liked her slow walk and drawl; when I saw her sitting among men, she seemed to me much too good to be among them; I would have given all their compliments if she would once have smiled at me as she smiled at them, with all her face breaking into radiance, with her dimples and flashing teeth. But I knew it never could be; I felt sure she hated me; that she wished I was dead; that she wished I had never come to the village. She did not know, when we went out riding, and a man who had always ridden beside her came to ride beside me, that I sent him away; that once when a man thought to win my favour by ridiculing her slow drawl before me I turned on him so fiercely that he never dared come before me again. I knew she knew that at the hotel men had made a bet as to which was the prettier, she or I, and had asked each man who came in, and that the one who had staked on me won. I hated them for it, but I would not let her see that I cared about what she felt towards me.

She and I never spoke to each other.

If we met in the village street we bowed and passed on; when we shook hands we did so silently, and did not look at each other. But I thought she felt my presence in a room just as I felt hers.

At last the time for my going came. I was to leave the next day. Some one I knew gave a party in my honour, to which all the village was invited.

It was midwinter. There was nothing in the gardens but a few dahlias and chrysanthemums, and I suppose that for two hundred miles round there was not a rose to be bought for love or money. Only in the garden of a friend of mine, in a sunny corner between the oven and the brick wall, there was a rose tree growing which had on it one bud. It was white, and it had been promised to the fair haired girl to wear at the party.

The evening came; when I arrived and went to the waiting-room, to take off my mantle, I found the girl there already. She was dressed in pure white, with her great white arms and shoulders showing, and her bright hair glittering in the candle-light, and the white rose fastened at her breast. She looked like a queen. I said "Good-evening," and turned away quickly to the glass to arrange my old black scarf across my old black dress.

Then I felt a hand touch my hair.

"Stand still," she said.

I looked in the glass. She had taken the white rose from her breast, and was fastening it in my hair.

"How nice dark hair is; it sets off flowers so." She stepped back and looked at me. "It looks much better there!"

I turned round.

"You are so beautiful to me," I said.

"Y-e-s," she said, with her slow Colonial drawl; "I'm so glad."

We stood looking at each other.

Then they came in and swept us away to dance. All the evening we did not come near to each other. Only once, as she passed, she smiled at me.

The next morning I left the town.

I never saw her again.

Years afterwards I heard she had married and gone to America; it may or may not be so—but the rose—the rose is in the box still! When my faith in woman grows dim, and it seems that for want of love and magnanimity she can play no part in any future heaven; then the scent of that small withered thing comes back:—spring cannot fail us.

Matjesfontein, South Africa.

III

THE POLICY IN FAVOUR OF PROTECTION—

Was it Right?—Was it Wrong?

A woman sat at her desk in the corner of a room; behind her a fire burnt brightly.

Presently a servant came in and gave her a card.

"Say I am busy and can see no one now. I have to finish this article by two o'clock."

The servant came back. The caller said she would only keep her a moment: it was necessary she should see her.

The woman rose from her desk. "Tell the boy to wait. Ask the lady to come in."

A young woman in a silk dress, with a cloak reaching to her feet, entered. She was tall and slight, with fair hair.

"I knew you would not mind. I wished to see you so!"

The woman offered her a seat by the fire. "May I loosen your cloak?—the room is warm."

"I wanted so to come and see you. You are the only person in the world who could help me! I know you are so large, and generous, and kind to other women!" She sat down. Tears stood in her large blue eyes: she was pulling off her little gloves unconsciously.

"You know Mr.—" (she mentioned the name of a well-known writer): "I know you meet him often in your work. I want you to do something for me!"

The woman on the hearth-rug looked down at her.

"I couldn't tell my father or my mother, or any one else; but I can tell you, though I know so little of you. You know, last summer he came and stayed with us a month. I saw a great deal of him. I don't know if he liked me; I know he liked my singing, and we rode together—I liked him more than any man I have ever seen. Oh, you know it isn't true that a woman can only like a man when he likes her; and I thought, perhaps, he liked me a little. Since we have been in town we have asked, but he has never come to see us. Perhaps people have been saying something to him about me. You know him, you are always meeting him, couldn't you say or do anything for me?" She looked up with her lips white and drawn. "I feel sometimes as if I were going mad! Oh, it is so terrible to be a woman!" The woman looked down at her. "Now I hear he likes another woman. I don't know who she is, but they say she is so clever, and writes. Oh, it is so terrible, I can't bear it."

The woman leaned her elbow against the mantelpiece, and her face against her hand. She looked down into the fire. Then she turned and looked at the younger woman. "Yes," she said, "it is a very terrible thing to be a woman." She was silent. She said with some difficulty: "Are you sure you love him? Are you sure it is not only the feeling a young girl has for an older man who is celebrated, and of whom every one is talking?"

"I have been nearly mad. I haven't slept for weeks!" She knit her little hands together, till the jewelled rings almost cut into the fingers. "He is everything to me; there is nothing else in the world. You, who are so great, and strong, and clever, and who care only for your work, and for men as your friends, you cannot understand what it is when one person is everything to you, when there is nothing else in the world!"

"And what do you want me to do?"

"Oh, I don't know!" She looked up. "A woman knows what she can do. Don't tell him that I love him." She looked up again. "Just say something to him. Oh, it's so terrible to be a woman;

I can't do anything. You won't tell him exactly that I love him? That's the thing that makes a man hate a woman, if you tell it him plainly."

"If I speak to him I must speak openly. He is my friend. I cannot fence with him. I have never fenced with him in my own affairs." She moved as though she were going away from the fireplace, then she turned and said: "Have you thought of what love is between a man and a woman when it means marriage? That long, long life together, day after day, stripped of all romance and distance, living face to face: seeing each other as a man sees his own soul? Do you realize that the end of marriage is to make the man and woman stronger than they were; and that if you cannot, when you are an old man and woman and sit by the fire, say, 'Life has been a braver and a freer thing for us, because we passed it hand in hand, than if we had passed through it alone,' it has failed? Do you care for him enough to live for him, not tomorrow, but when he is an old, faded man, and you an old, faded woman? Can you forgive him his sins and his weaknesses, when they hurt you most? If he were to lie a querulous invalid for twenty years, would you be able to fold him in your arms all that time, and comfort him, as a mother comforts her little child?" The woman drew her breath heavily.

"Oh, I love him absolutely! I would be glad to die, if only I could once know that he loved me better than anything in the world!"

The woman stood looking down at her. "Have you never thought of that other woman; whether she could not perhaps make his life as perfect as you?" she asked, slowly.

"Oh, no woman ever could be to him what I would be. I would live for him. He belongs to me." She bent herself forward, not crying, but her shoulders moving. "It is such a terrible thing to be a woman, to be able to do nothing and say nothing!"

The woman put her hand on her shoulder; the younger woman looked up into her face; then the elder turned away and stood looking into the fire. There was such quiet, you could hear the clock tick above the writing-table.

The woman said: "There is one thing I can do for you. I do not know if it will be of any use—I will do it." She turned away.

"Oh, you are so great and good, so beautiful, so different from other women, who are always thinking only of themselves! Thank you so much. I know I can trust you. I couldn't have told my mother, or any one but you."

"Now you must go; I have my work to finish."

The younger woman put her arms round her. "Oh, you are so good and beautiful!"

The silk dress and the fur cloak rustled out of the room.

The woman who was left alone walked up and down, at last faster and faster, till the drops stood on her forehead. After a time she went up to the table; there was written illegibly in a man's hand on a fragment of manuscript paper: "Can I come to see you this afternoon?" Near it was a closed and addressed envelope. She opened it. In it were written the words: "Yes, please, come."

She tore it across and wrote the words: "No, I shall not be at liberty."

She closed them in an envelope and addressed them. Then she rolled up the manuscript on the table and rang the bell. She gave it to the servant. "Tell the boy to give this to his master, and say the article ends rather abruptly; they must state it is to be continued; I will finish it tomorrow. As he passes No. 20 let him leave this note there."

The servant went out. She walked up and down with her hands folded above her head.

* * * * *

Two months after, the older woman stood before the fire. The door opened suddenly, and the younger woman came in.

"I had to come—I couldn't wait. You have heard, he was married this morning? Oh, do you think it is true? Do help me!"

She put out her hands.

"Sit down. Yes, it is quite true."

"Oh, it is so terrible, and I didn't know anything! Did you ever say anything to him?" She caught the woman's hands.

"I never saw him again after the day you were here,—so I could not speak to him,—but I did what I could." She stood looking passively into the fire.

"And they say she is quite a child, only eighteen. They say he only saw her three times before he proposed to her. Do you think it is true?"

"Yes, it is quite true."

"He can't love her. They say he's only marrying her for her rank and her money."

The woman turned quickly.

"What right have you to say that? No one but I know him. What need has he of any one's rank or wealth? He is greater than them all! Older women may have failed him; he has needed to turn to her beautiful, fresh, young life to compensate him. She is a woman whom any man might have loved, so young and beautiful; her family are famed for their intellect. If he trains her, she may make him a better wife than any other woman would have done."

"Oh, but I can't bear it—I can't bear it!" The younger woman sat down in the chair. "She will be his wife, and have his children."

"Yes." The elder woman moved quickly. "One wants to have the child, and lay its head on one's breast and feed it." She moved quickly. "It would not matter if another woman bore it, if one had it to take care of." She moved restlessly.

"Oh, no, I couldn't bear it to be hers. When I think of her I feel as if I were dying; all my fingers turn cold; I feel dead. Oh, you were only his friend; you don't know!"

The older spoke softly and quickly, "Don't you feel a little gentle to her when you think she's going to be his wife and the mother of his child? I would like to put my arms round her and touch her once, if she would let me. She is so beautiful, they say."

"Oh, I could never bear to see her; it would kill me. And they are so happy together today! He is loving her so!"

"Don't you want him to be happy?" The older woman looked down at her. "Have you never loved him, at all?"

The younger woman's face was covered with her hands. "Oh, it's so terrible, so dark! and I shall go on living year after year, always in this awful pain! Oh, if I could only die!"

The older woman stood looking into the fire; then slowly and measuredly she said, "There are times, in life, when everything seems dark, when the brain reels, and we cannot see that there is anything but death. But, if we wait long enough, after long, long years, calm comes. It may be we cannot say it was well; but we are contented, we accept the past. The struggle is ended. That day may come for you, perhaps sooner than you think." She spoke slowly and with difficulty.

"No, it can never come for me. If once I have loved a thing, I love it for ever. I can never forget."

"Love is not the only end in life. There are other things to live for."

"Oh, yes, for you! To me love is everything!"

"Now, you must go, dear."

The younger woman stood up. "It has been such a comfort to talk to you. I think I should have killed myself if I had not come. You help me so. I shall always be grateful to you."

The older woman took her hand.

"I want to ask something of you."

"What is it?"

"I cannot quite explain to you. You will not understand. But there are times when something more terrible can come into a life than it should lose what it loves. If you have had a dream of what life ought to be, and you try to make it real, and you fail; and something you have killed out in your heart for long years wakes up and cries, 'Let each man play his own game, and care nothing for the hand of his fellow! Each man for himself. So the game must be played!' and you doubt all you have lived for, and the ground seems washing out under your feet—." She paused. "Such a time has come to me now. If you would promise me that if ever another woman comes to seek your help, you will give it to her, and try to love her for my sake, I think it will help me. I think I should be able to keep my faith."

"Oh, I will do anything you ask me to. You are so good and great."

"Oh, good and great!—if you knew! Now go, dear."

"I have not kept you from your work, have I?"

"No; I have not been working lately. Good-by, dear."

The younger woman went; and the elder knelt down by the chair, and wailed like a little child when you have struck it and it does not dare to cry loud.

A year after; it was early spring again.

The woman sat at her desk writing; behind her the fire burnt brightly. She was writing a leading article on the causes which in differing peoples lead to the adoption of Free Trade or Protectionist principles.

The woman wrote on quickly. After a while the servant entered and laid a pile of letters on the table. "Tell the boy I shall have done in fifteen minutes." She wrote on. Then she caught sight of the writing on one of the letters. She put down her pen, and opened it. It ran so:—

> "DEAR FRIEND,—I am writing to you, because I know
> you will rejoice to hear of my great happiness. Do you
> remember how you told me that day by the fire to wait,
> and after long, long years I should see that all was for the
> best? That time has come sooner than we hoped. Last
> week in Rome I was married to the best, noblest, most
> large-hearted of men. We are now in Florence together.
> You don't know how beautiful all life is to me. I know now
> that the old passion was only a girl's foolish dream. My
> husband is the first man I have ever truly loved. He loves

me and understands me as no other man ever could. I am thankful that my dream was broken; God had better things in store for me. I don't hate that woman any more; I love every one! How are you, dear? We shall come and see you as soon as we arrive in England. I always think of you so happy in your great work and helping other people. I don't think now it is terrible to be a woman; it is lovely.

"I hope you are enjoying this beautiful spring weather.

"Yours, always full of gratitude and love,

"E—."

The woman read the letter: then she stood up and walked towards the fire. She did not re-read it, but stood with it open in her hand, looking down into the blaze. Her lips were drawn in at the corners. Presently she tore the letter up slowly, and watched the bits floating down one by one into the grate. Then she went back to her desk, and began to write, with her mouth still drawn in at the corners. After a while she laid her arm on the paper and her head on her arm, and seemed to go to sleep there.

Presently the servant knocked; the boy was waiting. "Tell him to wait ten minutes more." She took up her pen—"The Policy of the Australian Colonies in favour of Protection is easily understood—" she waited—"when one considers the fact—the fact—;" then she finished the article.

Cape Town, South Africa, 1892